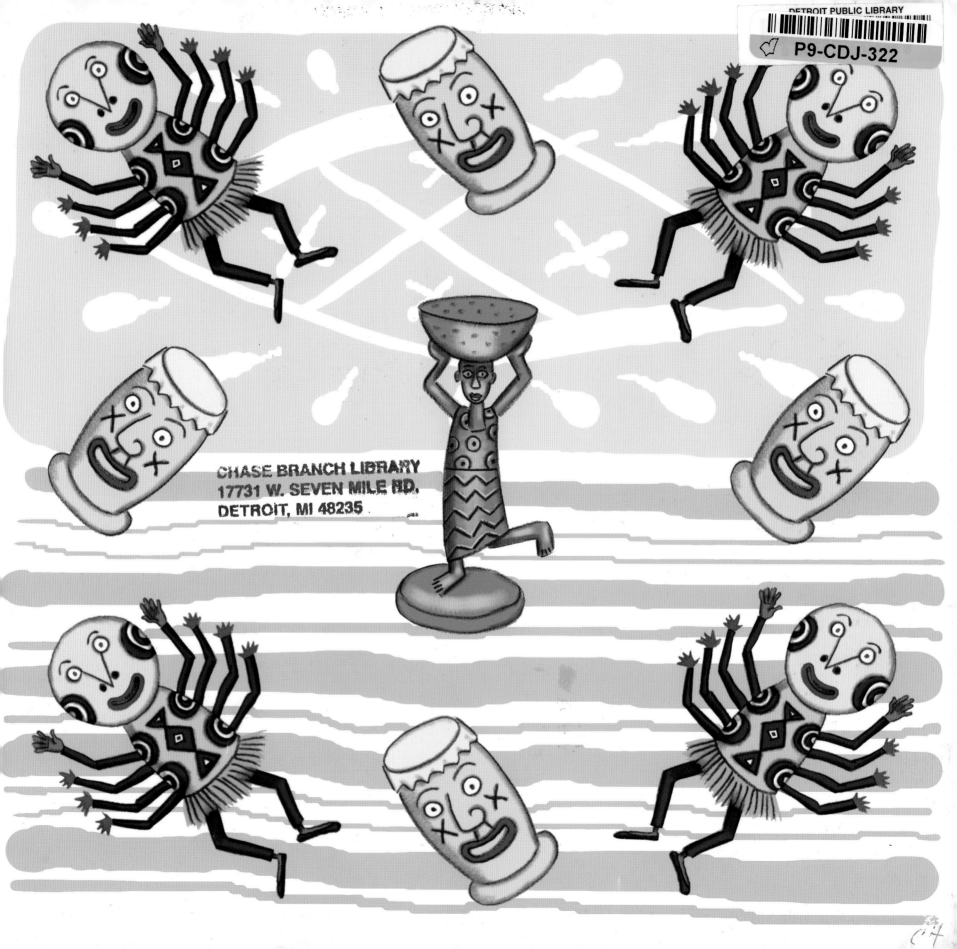

For Salma

Ghanaian words

ntama (n-TA-ma) is a wrap-around skirt.
atumpan (ah-TOOM-pon) is a talking drum.

Clarion Books
a Houghton Mifflin Company imprint
215 Park Avenue South, New York, NY 10003

Text and illustrations copyright © 2006 by Niki Daly
Cover and title page lettering designed by Sally Swart
First published in the United Kingdom in 2006 by Frances Lincoln Limited.
First American edition, 2007.

The illustrations were executed in watercolors and digital media.
The text was set in 15-point Bodoni.

www.houghtonmifflinbooks.com

Printed in Singapore

Library of Congress Cataloging-in-Publication Data

Daly, Niki.
Pretty Salma / by Niki Daly. — 1st American ed.
p. cm.
Summary: In this version of "Little Red Riding Hood," set in Ghana,
a young girl fails to heed Granny's warning about the dangers of talking to strangers.
ISBN-13: 978-0-618-72345-4
ISBN-10: 0-618-72345-5
[1. Fairy tales. 2. Folklore.] I. Title.
PZ8.D17Pr 2007
398.2—dc22
[E]
2006004249

FRL 10 9 8 7 6 5 4

Pretty Salma

A Little Red Riding Hood
Story from Africa

by Niki Daly

Clarion Books • New York

Salma lived with her granny and grandfather on the quiet side of town. One day, her granny said, "Salma! Pretty Salma, please go to market for your old granny, who loves you so."

Salma put on her blue scarf,

her stripy *ntama*,

her pretty white beads,

and her yellow sandals.

She tucked Granny's shopping list in her *ntama*, lifted Granny's big straw basket onto her head, and kissed Granny goodbye. "Straight there and back again!" said Granny. "And *don't* talk to strangers, you hear?"
"Okay, I promise," said Salma.

Off went Salma, *flip-flop, flip-flop* in her yellow sandals. As she walked, she sang her favorite song:

Oh, Salma, Pretty Salma,
Come kiss Granny,
your darling old Granny,
who loves you sooooooo!

At the market,
she bought

a giant watermelon,

a speckled rooster,

an ice-cold pink drink,
and a bunch of
candy-striped straws.

The sun was growing hot, and the basket
felt very heavy. So Salma decided to take a
shortcut home, through the wild side of town.

Along the way she sang her favorite song:

Oh, Salma, Pretty Salma,
Come kiss Granny,
your darling old Granny,
who loves you sooooooo!

"Are you Pretty Salma?"
asked a stranger.
It was Mr. Dog. He had been
listening to her song.
"Yes," said Salma.

"Are you going to Granny's?" asked Mr. Dog.
"Yes," said Salma.
"Well, your basket is much too heavy for
such a pretty little head," said Mr. Dog.
"Allow me to carry it for you."
Salma did feel a bit dizzy from the heat, so
she agreed to let Mr. Dog carry her basket.

The next day, Granny sent
Salma to market to buy
new clothes. Salma went
straight there and back.
And she never talked
to strangers again.

29

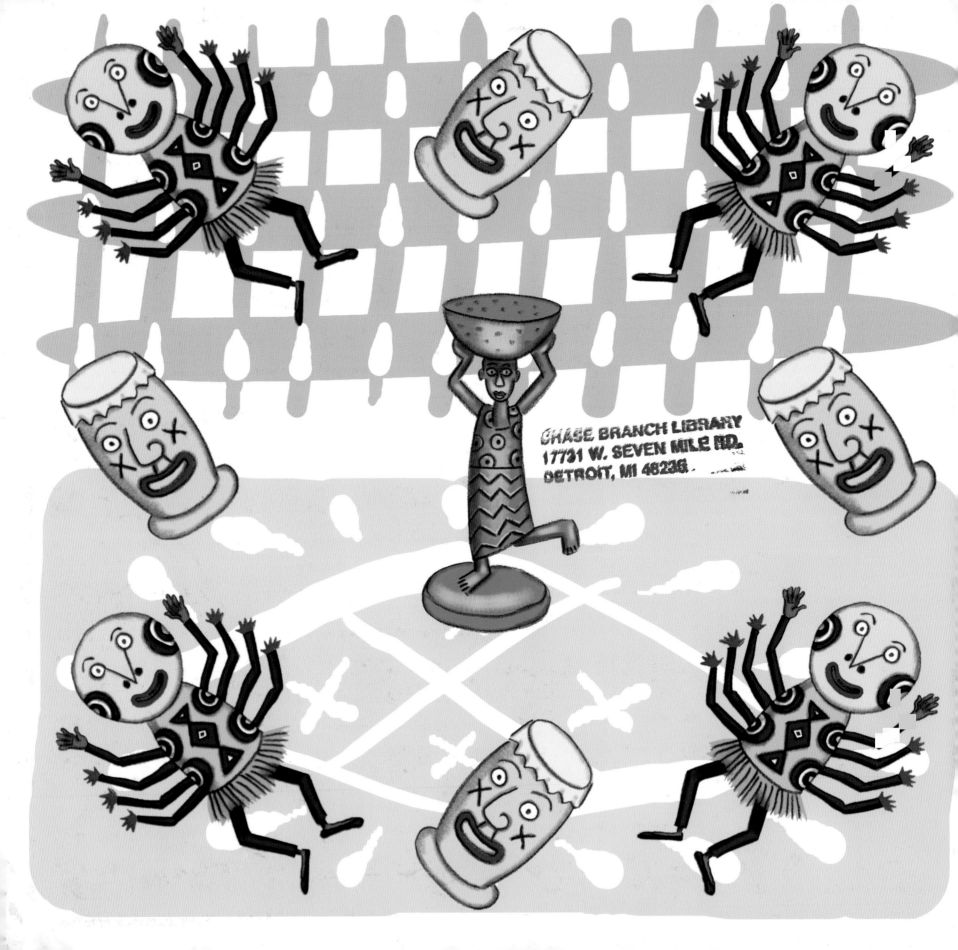